( To Peter

)

# FIREMAN SAM'S STORY TREASURY

## Fireman Sam
## and the Ring

story by Rob Lee
illustrations by the County Studio

DEAN

Sarah and James were going to call on Fireman Sam.
   "I hope Uncle Sam can take us swimming," said Sarah.
As they arrived, they noticed Penny's rescue tender, Venus,
parked outside.
   "Oh good!" said James. "Perhaps Penny can come as well."
The door was open so Sarah and James dashed straight in.

"Would you like to take us swimming, Uncle Sam?" asked Sarah.

"I'm afraid I'm working this afternoon," said Fireman Sam. "But I believe Penny might have plans for you."

"Swimming?" asked James hopefully.

"Not exactly," replied Penny.

Penny produced a large box from behind her back.

"What is it?" asked the twins.

"Open it and see," answered Penny. "It's a present."

James tore open the box. His eyes lit up.

"Brill!" he cried, admiring the bright red, remote control plane.

"Can we play with it now?" asked Sarah.

"I thought we'd give it a spin over the park," said Penny. "And then, if you're good, I may even treat you to an ice cream at Bella's cafe."

Fireman Sam waved goodbye and they all climbed into Penny's tender and drove off.

"I'll park here," said Penny, pulling up outside Bella's.

"Last one to the park's a cissy!" shouted Sarah as the twins. ran off.

"Don't worry about me," said Penny. "I'll just carry the plane."

Inside Bella's cafe, Bella was serving Trevor Evans. As she put his mug of tea in front of him Bella said, "How do you like my new ring, Trevor? It's a present from my great aunt Josefina, all the way from Italy."

Trevor stared at the hand Bella waved in front of his face.

"What ring, Bella?" he asked.

Bella looked at her hand and shrieked.

"My ring! It's gone!"

As Bella looked frantically for her ring, Trevor said, "Calm down, Bella! It must be here somewhere. What were you doing before you served me?"

"I was . . . washing up! That's it!" replied Bella.

"Well, it probably came off in the soapy water," said Trevor. "I bet my boots your ring's in the sink."

Bella searched in the washing-up bowl and all around the sink.

"It's not here," she sighed. "It probably fell down the plughole when I poured the dishwater away."

"Don't worry, Bella," soothed Trevor. "It's probably lodged in the pipes."

Trevor fetched his toolkit from the bus and unscrewed the plughole cover.

He tried to squeeze his hand in.

"My hand's too big," said Trevor. "You try, Bella."

Bella just managed to squeeze her hand into the plughole.
She waggled her fingers around inside the pipe.

"It's not at this end," she said after a while.

"Perhaps it's stuck further down," said Trevor, kneeling
down to inspect under the sink.

"This nut's stuck solid," he said, struggling to loosen it with
a spanner. "Not to worry, a little tap with my hammer should
do the trick."

Rosa appeared and looked on curiously as Trevor tapped the nut gently. Nothing happened. Trevor tapped a little harder. Suddenly the pipe came away from the wall and a jet of water spurted out straight into Trevor's face.

"Whaaaah!" he glugged. "Quick, Bella, grab a bucket!"

Rosa darted under a table in alarm.

Bella tried to move away, then looked at the sink in horror.

"I can't!" she groaned. "My hand's stuck down the plug-hole!"

Meanwhile in the park, James and Sarah were having difficulty starting the plane.

"If only Uncle Sam were here," sighed James. "He'd know what was wrong with it."

"I think we should be able to manage without your Uncle Sam," said Penny confidently, as she took a screwdriver from her top pocket.

"Yes, it looks like a jammed throttle to me," said Penny as she twiddled the screwdriver. She handed the plane back to James.

"That should do it," she said.

James twirled the propeller and the engine burst into life.

"Brill!" exclaimed James, very impressed.

Sarah pressed a button on the remote control and the plane flew off high into the sky.

"Look how fast it goes!" she cried.

"Let's see if I can make it do a loop the loop," said Sarah as she guided the joystick.

"Well done, Sarah," said Penny, watching the plane fly a perfect somersault.

"My turn," said James. "Watch this figure of eight."

"Bravo!" cried Penny. "Now try bringing it in to land."

Just then, however, the plane's engine coughed.

"What's wrong with it?" asked Sarah as the plane hiccuped and spluttered before diving down towards Bella's cafe.

"The controls aren't working," said James.

"It must be out of fuel," replied Penny. "Come on, let's get after it."

The twins followed Penny as she ran out of the park towards Bella's cafe.

Meanwhile, inside the cafe, Trevor was struggling with the water pipe, Bella still had her hand stuck in the plughole and the water level was rising fast.

"Do something, Trevor!" wailed Bella.

As the water got deeper and deeper, Rosa leapt onto a table.

"There must be a stopcock here somewhere," said Trevor as he groped under the water.

"No, it's . . . over there," said Bella, pointing to the other side of the cafe.

The water lapped around Trevor's waist as he searched on his hands and knees.

". . . Wait a minute," said Bella, "on second thoughts I think it's over there, or is it over . . ."

"On second thoughts, I think it would be a better idea to call the fire brigade," sighed Trevor.

"Good idea, Trevor," agreed Bella. "Phone the fire station."

"I will when I can find the phone," muttered Trevor. "Pity I never thought to bring a snorkel with me today."

Rosa leapt onto the counter as the water rose higher still. Cups and saucers floated past Trevor as he groped around.

"They look tasty," said Trevor hungrily, as a plate of cream cakes floated past his nose.

"Trevor!" cried Bella. "The phone!"

"Sorry, Bella," replied Trevor. "Ah, here it is."

He picked up the phone from under the water, only to see water dripping out of the receiver.

"Now we're sunk," he groaned.

Outside, Sarah, James and Penny were searching for their plane.

"It must be here somewhere," said James as he looked under Penny's rescue tender.

Sarah was looking outside Dilys Price's shop when Dilys appeared in the doorway.

"Well, what are you looking for?" she asked nosily.

"I'm looking for a plane," replied Sarah.

"You should try the airport," sniffed Dilys. "You won't find any planes around here."

"Yes, Dilys," sighed Sarah.

"Look, over here!" cried James from outside Bella's cafe.

"Have you found it?" asked Penny.

"No," he replied. "But Bella's cafe is leaking."

They saw a stream of water coming from under Bella's door. Sarah looked in the window.

"The cafe's flooded!" she cried.

When Penny opened the front door, a torrent of water rushed out past her, almost knocking her over.

"Quickly!" Penny called to the twins. "Phone the station! I'll see what I can do."

As the twins ran to the phone box Penny grabbed a stirrup pump from Venus.

Trevor was just about to join Rosa on the counter when Penny waded into the cafe.

"Bellissima!" cried Bella. "Thank goodness you've arrived, Penny."

"Right, Bella," said Penny. "First thing is the mains supply. Where's the stopcock?"

"It's, it's . . ." Bella hesitated. "Ah! I remember now, it's under the stairs."

"Well done," said Penny. "You'd be surprised at the people who don't know where their mains tap is."

"Really?" replied Bella innocently.

Trevor sighed.

Penny quickly shut off the water supply and began pumping out the cafe.

"Don't worry, Bella," she said. "I'll soon get rid of this water and then I'll see about freeing your hand."

"Good," said Trevor patting his tummy. "Because I'm ready for my breakfast."

"Not until you've helped me clear up, Trevor Evans," said Bella.

Sarah and James had phoned the station from the callbox in the square. Fireman Sam and Elvis Cridlington were polishing Jupiter when the call came through.

"Look lively, men!" shouted Station Officer Steele, reading the print-out. "Bella's cafe is flooded out!"

"Come on, Elvis!" called Fireman Sam as they grabbed their helmets and climbed aboard Jupiter. Fireman Sam switched on the sirens and they roared out of the station.

Sarah and James watched as Jupiter pulled in behind Venus.

"Looks like we've been beaten to it, Sir," said Fireman Sam to Station Officer Steele as they climbed down.

"Right, men," said Station Officer Steele, taking command. "Pumping equipment, at the double."

"Righto, Sir," replied Fireman Sam as he and Elvis unloaded the equipment and made for the cafe.

"What took you so long?" Penny teased the firemen when they appeared in the cafe doorway.

"Looks like most of the work's been done, Sir," said Fireman Sam.

"Good work, Firefighter Morris," said Station Officer Steele surveying the scene.

"What about me?" asked Bella, still trapped.

"You and Penny make sure the basement is pumped out," said Station Officer Steele to Elvis, "while Fireman Sam and I take care of Bella."

"Don't worry, Bella," said Fireman Sam. "I'll have you out of there in no time. Now let me see."

He found a bottle of washing-up liquid.

"A squirt of this and a drop of elbow grease should do the trick," said Fireman Sam.

He pulled Bella free and laughed, "That's a funny place to be putting your hand, Bella."

"I was looking for my new ring," explained Bella.

"I think that's gone for good," said Trevor.

"First I lose my great aunt Josefina's ring, then my beautiful cafe is ruined," wailed Bella.

"Don't worry," Fireman Sam reassured her. "As soon as we've packed up our equipment we'll help you clear up."

"I'll start mopping up, Sam," said Elvis.

"I'll help you," said Trevor.

"You're all so kind," said Bella.

"As soon as we've cleaned up I'll make a Bella Lasagne special espresso coffee for you all," said Bella.

"Just the job," replied Fireman Sam as he carried a pile of damp cardboard boxes out of the cafe. He was about to dump them in the rubbish bin in Bella's backyard when something caught his eye. "Well, well," he chuckled.

Soon the cafe was as clean as a new pin.

"Thank you so much," said Bella, serving everybody a steaming cup of coffee.

"That's one way of getting your cafe spring cleaned," chuckled Trevor as he put the usual four teaspoons of sugar into his coffee.

Trevor took a large swig of coffee and immediately began coughing and spluttering.

"Don't worry, Trev," said Fireman Sam and he patted him briskly on the back.

Suddenly Bella's ring popped out of Trevor's mouth onto the table.

"My ring!" cried Bella excitedly. "You've found it, Trevor!"

"It must have been in the sugar bowl all along," said Penny.

"In that case I'm surprised Trevor didn't find it before," laughed Fireman Sam.

As Bella admired the ring on her finger, Fireman Sam said to the twins,

"I've finished my shift now, perhaps you'd like to go swimming?"

"We've had enough water for one day," smiled Sarah.

"Just as well I was in Bella's backyard then," said Fireman Sam.

"Why's that, Uncle Sam?" asked James.

"Because I found this!" replied Fireman Sam.

He produced the twins' bright red plane.

"BRILL! Thanks Uncle Sam," they cried.

"Come on, Penny. Let's get back to the Park."

**FIREMAN SAM SAYS:**

Water can do a lot of damage. Be careful not to overfill sinks and baths and always turn off the taps before leaving a room.

# Fireman Sam
# and the Bonfire

story by Diane Wilmer
illustrations by the County Studio

Sarah and James were playing football in Fireman
Sam's back garden.
   "Watch out for my windows," laughed Fireman Sam.
   "And for my washing," called Trevor Evans. "I've
just washed my best shirt."

"We'll be careful," promised Sarah.

"It's my birthday today and Bella's invited me round for supper," said Trevor. "So I've got to look extra-specially smart tonight."

"We won't dirty your clean shirt," promised James.

Sarah kicked the ball to James. WHACK! It bounced
past him and landed on top of Fireman Sam's
rubbish heap.

"Bother!" said Sarah. "Now what do we do?"

"We'll have to get it down," said James.

"How?" asked Sarah.

James looked around. "Maybe I can get it down
with the rake," he said.

He poked the top of the heap with the long rake and the ball came tumbling down. So did Fireman Sam's rubbish heap.

"We'd better tidy it up a bit," said Sarah.

"All right," agreed James.

They started to pile up the fallen wood.

Suddenly, something flashed past James.

"Oh! What was that?" he cried.

"I don't know," said Sarah. "I think it ran under the rubbish heap."

They peeped inside the tangled heap. It was musty and dark.

"I can't see anything," said Sarah.

"Wait," hissed James. "Look, there! Something's moving."

Sarah stared hard. "It's a little mouse!" she cried.

"Ssshhhsh!" whispered James. "Let's see where it goes."

The mouse scurried into a bundle of leaves and
dried grass. Lots of tiny mice started to wriggle
around her.

"She's got babies!" squeaked Sarah.

"Come away," said James. "We don't want to
frighten them."

"All right," said Sarah. "Let's tidy the heap and
then leave them alone."

They picked up their ball and crept to the end of
the garden.

"Shall we tell Uncle Sam?" said James.

"No," said Sarah. "Let's keep it a secret."

They went indoors to have some lemonade with
Fireman Sam.

A moment later, Trevor Evans came out to take his washing off the line. "Mmmm, my shirt's still a bit damp," he said. "I'll leave it out while I pop to the shops, then I'll iron it when I get back."

Sarah and James finished their drink then offered to go shopping for Fireman Sam.

"I'll have a loaf of brown bread and a jar of peanut butter, please, and there'll be enough change left for two ice-creams," he smiled.

"Thanks, Uncle Sam!" cried James and Sarah, and they ran off down the road.

Fireman Sam finished weeding his flower bed then swept the garden path and put all the rubbish in his wheelbarrow. He pushed it round to the back garden and piled all the rubbish onto the heap.

"Goodness, I'll have to do something about this lot," gasped Fireman Sam. "Maybe I'll light a bonfire to get rid of it."

He looked over the fence to see whether Trevor had taken in his washing. The line looked empty.

"I think I'll light the fire now, while Trevor's out," thought Fireman Sam. "Then he won't be bothered by the smoke."

He didn't notice the shirt still on the line in a corner of the garden. And he didn't know anything about the family of mice living in the rubbish heap.

Down in Pontypandy, Trevor was chatting to Bella
inside her cafe, while the twins were eating their
ice-creams outside Dilys's shop and chatting to
Norman, Dilys's son.

"Look up there," yelled Norman, suddenly.
"Fireman Sam's garden is on fire!"

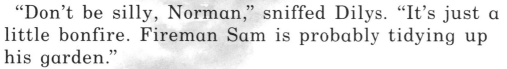

"Don't be silly, Norman," sniffed Dilys. "It's just a little bonfire. Fireman Sam is probably tidying up his garden."

Sarah dropped her ice-cream.

"A bonfire!" she cried. "Oh no!"

"We've got to stop him!" yelled James.

When Trevor heard all the shouting he ran across the road.

"What's going on?" he asked.

"Uncle Sam's lit a bonfire in his garden," said Sarah.

"And there's a mouse in it, with lots of little babies," said James.

"Oh no!" yelled Trevor. "And what about my best shirt?"

They ran up the hill to the fire station and Sarah rang the fire bell. RING-A-LING-LING!

Fireman Elvis Cridlington came running to the door, wiping tomato ketchup off his face.

"Hey! What's up?" he asked.

"There's a fire in Fireman Sam's garden," said Trevor.

"And we've got to put it out," cried James.

"It's an emergency!" yelled Sarah.

Elvis jumped into Jupiter's driving seat and
switched on the siren.

"Right Fireman Cridlington," said Fire Officer
Steele. "Off we go."

Fireman Sam looked up when he heard Jupiter's
siren wailing.

"Goodness me! I wonder what's on fire?" he worried.

He couldn't believe his eyes when Jupiter stopped
right outside his own house!

"Elvis!" called Fireman Sam. "What's wrong?"

"FIRE!" cried Elvis.

"We've got to put out your bonfire, Fireman Sam,"
said Fire Officer Steele.

"Quick! Quick!" shouted James and Sarah as they
rushed up the hill.

Elvis came running up the path with the fire hose
and Fire Officer Steele turned on the water.

"Stop! What *is* going on?" shouted Fireman Sam.

"Sorry Sir," gasped Elvis. "I'll explain later. This is
a real emergency!"

The water came spurting through the nozzle and
Elvis aimed it at the bonfire. WHOOOOSH! In
seconds the fire was out.

"That's done it," said Elvis.

"It certainly has," snapped Fireman Sam. "Now, will somebody please tell me what you're doing with that hose?"

"There's a mouse living in the bonfire, Uncle Sam," said Sarah.

"She had a nest under there," said James. "With lots of babies in it."

"Oh dear," said Fireman Sam. "Why didn't you tell me?"
"We wanted to keep it a secret," said Sarah.
Trevor came marching up.
"I'm furious, Fireman Sam!" he roared. "You're
supposed to be a good neighbour. Didn't you see my
shirt hanging on the washing line."

"Of course I didn't," cried Fireman Sam. "I looked over the fence and I couldn't see it!"

"I left it in the corner," moaned Trevor.

"No wonder I couldn't see it," said Fireman Sam.

"Hmmm!" sniffed Trevor. "Now I'll have to wash it all over again!"

Trevor stomped off to look at his shirt. Fireman Sam and the twins poked around underneath the dripping bonfire. There was no sign of the mouse or her babies.

"Where can she be?" asked Sarah.

"I don't know," said Fireman Sam. "But I *do* know I wish I'd never lit that bonfire."

"So do I," muttered Trevor, from over the fence. "Just look at my best shirt. Now what will I wear to Bella's tonight?" snapped Trevor and crossly kicked at the leaves around his rhubarb plant.

"SQUEAK! SQUEAK! SQUEAK! SQUEAK!"

"It's the mice!" cried James. "They must have escaped into Trevor's garden when Uncle Sam lit the bonfire."

They hurried round to Trevor's garden and rushed up the path.

"Quiet now," warned Trevor. "We don't want to frighten them again."

Fireman Sam bent down and very gently lifted up the big green rhubarb leaves. Tucked underneath them was an old watering can, full of leaves and snuggled inside it was the mouse with all her babies.

"They're safe," whispered Sarah.

"Safe as houses," said Fireman Sam.

"Well I never," laughed Trevor. "I've been wondering where that old watering can was!"

"Come on, let's leave them alone," said Fireman Sam. "I think they've had enough excitement for one day."

"I must take Jupiter back to the Fire Station," said Elvis, rolling up the hose.

"Hold on a minute, we'll come with you," called Fireman Sam. "I want to pop into Bella's."

"You can tell her I'll be late," said Trevor.

They left him behind, washing his shirt for the second time that day.

Elvis dropped them off outside Bella's cafe and the three of them walked in. They found Bella icing Trevor's birthday cake.

"His favourite cake," said Bella. "Chocolate cream, with fudge filling. He will love it, I know."

"I'm sure he will," said Fireman Sam, nervously. "But he'll be a bit late. Er . . . you see Bella, there's been a bit of an accident."

"Accident!" cried Bella. "What happened? Is Trevor all right?"

"Yes," said Sarah. "But his best shirt isn't."

"He washed it," explained James. "So he'd look extra-specially smart for you tonight."

"But I didn't see it hanging on the line," said Fireman Sam. "And I lit a bonfire and blew smoke all over it."

"He's washing his shirt again, and he asked us to tell you he'll be late," said James.

Bella burst out laughing. "Oh! You mustn't worry!"
she chuckled. "Just look what I've bought him for
his birthday."

She held up a shiny packet and they all stared at it.

"A new shirt!" cried Fireman Sam.

"A beautiful shirt!" laughed Bella. "Here, James
and Sarah, take this to Trevor and tell him to come
quickly. His birthday supper is ready and waiting!"

## FIREMAN SAM SAYS :

Bonfires can be a nuisance. Before a
grown-up lights one, they should make sure
it won't annoy the neighbours.

# Fireman Sam
# and the Fountain

story by Diane Wilmer
illustrations by the County Studio

Pontypandy Park had been open for a hundred years.
  "It's the centenary next week," said Station Officer Steele.
"We must do something really special to celebrate the event."
  "Bella's organised a party," said Fireman Sam.
  "Hmm," said Station Officer Steele. "We need something
extra special, that no one else will have thought of."

"I've got it!" said Fireman Sam. "We can mend the fountain in the park. You know, the one in the middle, just near the bandstand. It's not worked for years. We could get it going and paint it up, it'd look a real treat."

"Jolly good," said Station Officer Steele. "Let's get cracking, we've not a minute to waste."

The day of the centenary came and it was boiling hot.

"PHEW!" gasped Fireman Elvis Cridlington as he buttoned up his heavy uniform. "I could do with a swim."

"Not now, Cridlington," said Station Officer Steele. "Let's just concentrate on the fountain for the moment."

"Well, I hope it works," said Fireman Sam as he oiled up the old pump.

"Of course it'll work, it just needs a bit of organisation!" said Station Officer Steele. "Cridlington will be here, in the control shed. You'll be standing at the back of the crowd and after I've given my speech and cut the ribbon tied around the fountain, you'll wave to Cridlington and he'll turn on the water. Easy as blinking!"

"It's not quite that simple, Sir," said Fireman Sam.

"Some of these workings are pretty old, they might jam after all these years."

"Nonsense!" laughed Station Officer Steele. "Everything will be fine!"

The band played and people began to wander up the hill to the park.

"Come on, James!" called Sarah. "Or we'll be late for the opening ceremony."

"Quick!" yelled Norman, "Station Officer Steele is just about to start his speech."

"Hum . . . hum . . . hum . . . hum!" said Station Officer Steele. "Thank you all for coming to the opening of the Park Fountain. My men and I have worked very hard to restore it and we hope that you will be as proud of it as we are!" He cut the red ribbon and smiled.

"I now declare this fountain well and truly open!"

"Hurray! Hurray!" cheered the children.

"Well done, boys!" cried Trevor Evans.

"There's beautiful," smiled Dilys.

Fireman Sam gave the thumbs up sign to Elvis, who turned the wheel – but nothing happened.

"Er . . . I now declare this fountain, er, well and truly . . . OPEN!" yelled Station Officer Steele. Still nothing happened. "What's going on?" he hissed.

Fireman Sam shrugged his shoulders. "I don't know but I'll try and find out," he said.

He found Elvis struggling with the big wheel.

"What's up?" he asked.

"The bloomin' thing's jammed," said Elvis. "I can't move it."

"Give it a bash with your hammer," said Fireman Sam. "That should shift it alright."

"OK," said Elvis and whacked the wheel with his hammer. C–L–A–N–G!

Meanwhile Station Officer Steele was peering into the centre of the fountain.

"Just hold on," he was saying. "I'll soon have this sorted out."

*Whoooosh!* The water came shooting up and hit him smack in the face.

"Well, that's one way of cooling off!" said Trevor Evans.

"Can we all join in?" asked Norman.

"Certainly not!" dripped Station Officer Steele. "The fountain's only for fish."

Norman peered into the big, stone bowl. "I can't see any fish," he said.

"They're here," said James and he tipped some goldfish out of a plastic bag into the water.

"Where did they come from?" asked Norman.

"From the pond," said Sarah. "Look I've got some too." She tipped her bag into the water and with a flick of their tails the fish went darting off.

"Quack! Quack!" went some ducks and landed with a splash in the fountain.

Norman watched the ducks. "I'd like a paddle too," he thought and hid behind the bushes.

The band began to play and everyone slowly wandered over to the bandstand to listen to the music.

"Are you coming down to my party later?" Bella asked the firemen.

"We'll be down when we've finished this shift," said Fireman Sam.

"Where's Norman?" asked Sarah.

"He's probably run on ahead to sample the ice-cream!" laughed Trevor.

As soon as they'd all gone Norman slipped out from his hiding place and jumped into the fountain.

"Whoopee!" he cried as he danced in and out of the splashing water. "Cool at last...wheeee!"

Suddenly he heard a voice.

"Hello there Norman! I thought you'd gone back to Bella's?"

"*Ooh*, Elvis!" gulped Norman. "What are you doing here?"

"I had to stay behind and fix this bloomin' fountain," said Elvis. "But look what I found..." He held up an old football. "Here – catch!" The ball came whizzing towards Norman who caught it and sent it flying back to Elvis. Then Elvis kicked it really high. It landed, PLOP, right on top of the fountain.

"WOW! What a shot!" giggled Norman.

"Oh dear, it's stuck up there," said Elvis.

"Don't worry, I'll get it," said Norman.

But the ball was slowly slipping down inside the fountain-head.

"Quick, grab it!" yelled Elvis.

GLUG! went the ball and disappeared down the pipe.

"Well, that's the end of that," said Elvis. "Better not tell anybody, Norman or we'll both be in trouble."

"OK, mum's the word," said Norman, pressing his finger to his lips.

"Mum's the word," said Elvis with a wink.

When Elvis arrived back at the Fire Station, he had to clean all the windows.

"Well, at least it's a cool job," he thought. "Better be quick though, or I'll miss all the fun down in Pontypandy."

Station Officer Steele was thinking the same thing. "I'll finish my filing then go down to Bella's," he thought, but his room was very hot. "PHEW!" he gasped and threw open the window. He stood there, trying to cool down, when along came Elvis, singing at the top of his voice.

Without looking up, Elvis picked up his bucket of water and whizzed it straight at the window – *whooosh!* The water went flying and hit Station Officer Steele right in the face.

"AAAGHH!" he roared.

Elvis dropped his bucket and started to tremble.

"Oh my giddy aunt!" he gulped. "I... er... I thought the window was shut!"

"Well it wasn't!" cried Station Officer Steele. "This is the second time you've drenched me today."

"It was an accident," said Elvis. "I promise it won't ever happen again."

"Hummmph! Well just make sure it doesn't," said Station Officer Steele. "Otherwise you'll be in big trouble, Fireman Cridlington. Now hurry up and get those windows finished, at the double!"

Down at Bella's cafe the party was in full swing.

"Delicious!" said Trevor, tucking into more sandwiches.

"Now, now, Trevor, don't eat everything," scolded Dilys. "The firemen haven't arrived yet."

"Come on," said Sarah to James. "Let's go up to the park and have a look at our fish."

It was quiet in the park and very, very hot.

"That's funny," said James as they walked along the path. "I can't hear the fountain. It was quite loud when we left."

Sarah stood still and listened. "I can't hear anything either," she said.

They stared at each other, thinking exactly the same thing. "The FISH!" they cried and ran to the fountain.

They found the fish flopping about in a tiny bit of water, all that was left in the bottom of the big, stone bowl.

"Quick," said James. "We must scoop them out and put them in the pond."

"Oh dear," said Sarah. "Do you think they'll be all right?"

The fish were still for a while then they slowly began to move around the pond.

"They're fine," said James. "But I think we'd better tell Uncle Sam about the fountain."

"Poor Uncle Sam, he'll be really fed up," said Sarah. "He's been working all day."

Fireman Sam *was* fed up. "Oh daro!" he said. "I was just about to leave for Bella's party."

"I'd better come with you," said Station Officer Steele. "Elvis is still busy cleaning the windows."

They climbed into Jupiter and Fireman Sam drove them down the hill to the park.

"Hey! Where are you going?" yelled Elvis.

"To the park," said Station Officer Steele. "The fountain's blocked up again."

"Again?" said Elvis, then he remembered. "Oh no, the ball!" he cried. "HEY! Wait for me!"

But it was too late. Fireman Sam had turned the corner and was thundering down the hill to Pontypandy.

"HELP!" spluttered Elvis. "If Station Officer Steele finds that ball, there'll be big trouble!"

Fireman Sam and Station Officer Steele were very puzzled.

"I don't know what the problem is," said Fireman Sam. "I've checked everything. The blockage must be up top."

Station Officer Steele peered into the fountain-head. "I can't see a thing down there," he said.

"I'll tell you what, Sir," said Fireman Sam. "I'll switch the pump onto maximum and see if that helps."

They all waited while Fireman Sam turned up the pump, but nothing happened.

"What's going on?" called Station Officer Steele.

"I don't know," answered Fireman Sam. "I'll pump up more water, maybe the increased water pressure will push the blockage through."

Again they waited but still nothing happened.

"It's well and truly blocked this time," said James.

"It's very strange," said Fireman Sam. "The water's going through all right, I can hear it loud and clear, but it's not coming out the other end."

Suddenly a loud rumble came from the control shed.

"Uh-oh!" cried Fireman Sam. "Sounds like we've got problems." He grabbed the wheel to turn the water off, but as he turned it the wheel broke off in his hands.

At that moment Elvis came racing up the hill towards them. "Stop!" he gasped. "S T O P!"

But nobody was listening to him. The rumble changed to a roar as the water thundered through the pipes.

"Oh, Uncle Sam!" cried Sarah. "What's happening?"

"The pressure's building up," said Fireman Sam. "It's got to come up somewhere."

"Yes, but WHERE is the question," said Station Officer Steele.

Suddenly a manhole cover just beneath the bandstand shot up into the air. WHOOOOSH! The water came bubbling up in a great fountain.

"Stand clear! Stand clear!" yelled Fireman Sam.

There was no stopping the water. It rushed out of the pipes down the path, straight towards Pontypandy.

Elvis ran over to the fountain. "It's OK," he said. "I can fix it."
He climbed onto the fountain and reached down inside it.

"Got it!" he cried, pulling out the ball with a loud POP!

"This is no time for silly games, Cridlington," said Station
Officer Steele. "Just what do you think you're up to?"

"I'll explain later," said Elvis and quickly jumped down.
"Watch out, here it comes!"

The water came shooting up out of the fountain and
splashed into the stone bowl.

"Thank goodness for that," said Fireman Sam. "Now give me a hand with the manhole cover."

They all helped Fireman Sam lift the heavy lid and put it back over the manhole.

"Is it safe Uncle Sam?" asked Sarah.

"It's safe now," said Fireman Sam. "The water from the fountain has taken the pressure off the pipes. We'll have everything back to normal in no time."

"But what about the wheel?" asked James. "Won't you have to mend it?"

"Yes, I'll have to get some welding equipment from the fire station," said Fireman Sam. "I'll come and mend it later."

"Come on," said Station Officer Steele. "Let's go down to Pontypandy and see if any damage has been done."

In the village they found the main street awash.

"*WHHEEE!* This is great!" cried Norman as he splashed about. "Just like the seaside."

"Norman, get out of the way," said Station Officer Steele. "We've got to pump this lot up."

Elvis got the hoses out. He put one into the water and the other into the river.

"Rightio," he called. "Switch on the pump."

Fireman Sam operated the controls, as one of the hoses sucked in the water and the other pumped it out into the river. In no time the street was clear.

"Well done!" called Dilys.

"Jolly good!" boomed Trevor Evans.

"Bravo!" cried Bella.

"Now Elvis, perhaps you'd like to tell me about the football in the fountain?" said Station Officer Steele.

Elvis looked uncomfortable. "Well," he said. "Norman and I were having a game of football earlier on this afternoon and the ball sort of . . . er . . ."

"Got stuck on top of the fountain," continued Norman.

"Got stuck!" snapped Station Officer Steele. "You were on duty, Cridlington. What were you doing playing football?"

"Oh! it wasn't him," interrupted Norman. "It was me that kicked the ball. He just kicked it back."

"And when he kicked it back it went straight inside the fountain?" asked Fireman Sam. "You were never much good at football, were you, Elvis?"

Norman giggled, but Station Officer Steele looked annoyed.

"Come on, let's not argue today," smiled Bella and led the way into her cafe.

"Look, all your favourite things," she said.

"Mmmm . . . this is lovely," said Fireman Sam.

"Phew! I thought I was in trouble then," whispered Elvis.

Norman winked and pressed his finger to his lips. "Mum's the word," he said.

"Have you tried my spicy pizza?" Bella asked Station Officer Steele.

"No, but I'd certainly like to," he replied.

"Watch out for it," warned Trevor Evans. "It's a bit on the hot side."

"Oh, that won't worry me," said Station Officer Steele and he bit into the pizza. "AAAAGHHH!" he cried. "Water! Water!"

Elvis grabbed a glass of water and handed it to Station Officer Steele.

"Water, Sir," he said. "There's plenty of that in Pontypandy!"

## FIREMAN SAM SAYS:

Football is a good game but only play in wide open spaces where you won't break anything if you miss the ball.

This edition first published in Great Britain 1995
by Dean, an imprint of Reed Children's Books
Michelin House, 81 Fulham Road, London SW3 6RB
and Auckland, Melbourne, Singapore and Toronto

This edition copyright © Reed International Books Ltd 1995

Fireman Sam copyright © 1985 Prism Art & Design Limited
*Fireman Sam and the Ring* copyright © Reed International Books Ltd 1990
*Fireman Sam and the Bonfire* copyright © Reed International Books Ltd 1988
*Fireman Sam and the Fountain* copyright © Reed International Books Ltd 1990
All rights reserved
Based on the animation series produced by Bumper Films
for S4C/Channel 4 Wales and Prism Art & Design Limited
Original idea by Dave Gingell and Dave Jones assisted by
Mike Young. Characters created by Rob Lee.
Stories by Rob Lee and Diane Wilmer
Illustrations by County Studio

ISBN 0 603 55415 6

Produced by Mandarin Offset Ltd
Printed and bound in Hong Kong